For Colten, my favorite first grandson

and

Poppy, the love of my life.

AuthorHouse™
1663 Liberty Drive
Bloomington, IN 47403
www.authorhouse.com
Phone: 1 (800) 839-8640

Published by AuthorHouse 12/20/2018

ISBN: 978-1-5462-7301-1 (sc)
ISBN: 978-1-5462-7300-4 (e)

Library of Congress Control Number 2018914884

Print information available on the last page.

Any people depicted in stock imagery provided by Getty Images are models,
and such images are being used for illustrative purposes only.
Certain stock imagery © Getty Images.

This book is printed on acid-free paper.

authorHOUSE®

Colten
and the Bullfrog
the Adventure

Julie Houston Rogers

Illustrated by Joshua Allen

One morning, before the sun woke up, Colten got Poppy out of bed to go watch the old bullfrog that lives in Mema's fish pond. He couldn't wait to lay his eyes on that "old man," as Poppy called him. Poppy grabbed the flashlight and his cap, and Colten grabbed *his* cap, just like Poppy. And then out the back door they went. They were ready for their first big adventure, and Colten could already hear the call of the wild. He was mighty impatient, waiting for Poppy to decide on just the right time to move out!

They sat down on the swing, and Poppy explained, "When you are in the wild, you must remember some very important points if you want to be a successful and observant nature watcher. First, you must be patient. You must be willing to wait for what you want. Wait for the thrill!"

"Secondly, you absolutely must be quiet. Strange noises or noises that are out of place will frighten what you are waiting for, and you will never see it! This means no talking!"

Colten thought, *"Boy, my cousin Elee would really be in trouble; she cannot stop talking!"*

"Lastly, you must sit still! Absolutely no fidgeting!"

Once he had shared all this information, Poppy asked, "Do you have any questions, Colten?"

"Well, no, Poppy, not right now, but we haven't done anything yet!"

It was still dark as they moved off the porch. Colten could hear the chirping of the crickets in the grass and thought they were terribly loud that morning. He guessed being this close to them made it seem that way. The birds were already stirring and beginning to sing from the big old pecan trees in Poppy's backyard. He could even hear the gurgling sound of running water in Mema's fishpond.

Then, suddenly, he heard the strangest sound coming from the water. "Mmwww, rrriiiiddiit, mmwwwwwww!" It was definitely a scary sound.

Poppy fixed the flashlight so it wouldn't shine in the water and scare the noise away. It was a good thing he did, because if whatever made that sound did it again, someone would be running scared, and it wouldn't be Poppy!

Then, there it was, as big as day. That bullfrog! He was floating in the pond as if he owned the place. He sang out loud and clear as he moved from side to side.

"Poppy, does he always make that sound?" Colten whispered.

"Yes, Colten, he always makes that sound. That is the way he communicates and lets other frogs know he is here," he whispered.

"Poppy, where do bullfrogs go in the morning?" Colten didn't think he'd ever seen one during the day!

"Well, Colten, bullfrogs tend to lead a quiet life during the daytime. While they hunt at night, you might see them sunbathing on the rocks or sometimes even hunting during the day. When the sun is way up in the sky, the bullfrog might be found hiding under vegetation, beneath a large, shady leaf such as that of an elephant ear plant. He might also be under overhanging banks at the water's edge or resting in shallow water such as Mema's fish pond.

They got down on their knees to observe without being seen. With the flashlight, they were able to see the bullfrog's legs stretched out under the water. He was so relaxed; he looked as if he was floating on the waves of an ocean. He was trying to hide in the cattails and water lilies growing there. Poppy covered the light so they could watch him without being seen.

Suddenly, that bullfrog turned and climbed from the pond onto the rocks.

Once again that loud, scary sound began. It was soft at first, but then it was loud enough to scare away the bravest creature.

"Mmmmmmmwwwwww, rrrriiiiiddiitttt, mmmww, mmww!" He sang louder and even louder still.

"Ridit, ridit, jug-o-rum!"

He was king of the hill, proud and noble. He stared quietly, almost as if it was his last time surveying all that was his. His tiny kingdom! He looked around for a while, and then, just before dawn, the old man hopped silently into the tall elephant ears planted near the pond.

"Poppy, why does he sing that song?"

"He sings the song to let other male frogs know that he has claimed this pond and will willingly fight for it. That, in turn, attracts the female bullfrogs."

"Why did the bullfrog go away?"

"Well, Colten, there are some things you should know about bullfrogs. They are nocturnal, which means they stay awake all night. Old Man Bullfrog claims this pond as his own. Bullfrogs don't like to share and will fight for what they believe belongs to them. So, when the sun goes down, he will come out to sing his brave song and swim in his pond. This pond will remain his until a stronger bullfrog claims it. The bullfrog goes away when the sun comes up because it is time to rest! Usually, they hide and wait for dark, and then they come out again to claim their territory.

Next, bullfrogs are carnivores and eat almost anything, anything meat, that is! They will eat fish, small birds, mammals, and even other frogs. Using their sticky tongues, bullfrogs will snatch their prey into their mouths and with their sharp teeth, keep them there.

Lastly, bullfrogs are amphibians! The word amphibian means "double life". That means these animals need both land and water during their life cycle. They begin their lives as clumps of eggs living on the surface of the water. Then they become tadpoles, living in the water with slimy, slippery, thin skin. As adults, they lose their tails and gills, but their skin remains thin and moist. So they can keep their skin cool and moist, they live close to ponds, marshes, swamps, and any other fresh water source. Remember, they must not dehydrate so they cannot live in salt water.

They stood, Colten's feet aching terribly from being down for so long. They went back to the porch, where they sat on the steps and waited for the sky to finish its early-morning light show.

They leaned back and watched silently as the sky lightened even more. They were both mulling over their thoughts when the smell of bacon frying crossed Colten's nose. He knew Mema would have breakfast waiting and would be anxious to hear all about their bullfrog adventure.

"Let's go eat, Poppy!" shouted Colten.

They stood slowly, as if both their bodies were that of old men. And as if they were thinking the same thing, Poppy said, "Old Man Bullfrog sure has a lot to take care of living in that pond of Mema's."

"He sure does, Poppy," Colten said, laughing, as they joined Mema in the kitchen for some fried bacon, some funny stories, and who knows what other good things to eat and talk about.

Fun Facts:

- The female bullfrog can lay as many as twenty thousand eggs, which float in a clump on the surface of the water.

- Bullfrogs begin as a mass of floating eggs that become tadpoles and later transform into froglets.

- The development of bullfrogs is slow. It takes from one to three years to begin transformation from the tadpole stage into the adult stage.

- Tadpoles can reach up to 6.75 inches in length. Adult frogs grow to be eight inches or more in length.

- They can weigh up to 1.5 pounds and are about the size of a teacup.

- Frogs are amphibians; they have sticky tongues that trap prey in their mouths, where sharp teeth are used to hold them.

- The frogs' habitats include lakes, ponds, rivers, bogs, streams, marshes, and swamps. Warm, calm, shallow waters are their favorite places.

- They hibernate in the winter by making caves in the shallow waters of their habitat.

- A frog's call, which is very much like that of a cow, can be heard from half a mile away.

About the Author

Julie Houston Rogers, a retired fifth-grade teacher, has always loved reading and making up stories to share with children. So she decided to write stories for children about history and science. She lives in a small South Georgia town with her husband, Doyle; her Yorkie, Lucy Loo; and two cats, Spanky and Bitsy. Their three children, Buck, Cody, and Beki have always said their home was as wild and funny as a TV comedy. So, they left home when they were ready to start their *own* sitcom.

Lightning Source UK Ltd.
Milton Keynes UK
UKHW051328030119
334908UK00006B/45/P